Contents

*With love and thanks to seven **special**
people for the privilege and fun of
being their mum*

Pins and Needles

JANET SLATER BOTTIN

Illustrated by Toni Goffe

Scripture Union

The author acknowledges with thanks a literary grant from the Arts Council of New Zealand.

© Janet Slater Bottin 2000
First published 2000

Scripture Union, 207–209 Queensway, Bletchley, Milton Keynes, MK2 2EB, England.

ISBN 1 85999 395 8

British Library Cataloguing-in-Publication Data.
A catalogue record of this book is available from the British Library.

All illustrations by Toni Goffe.

Printed and bound in Great Britain by
Creative Print and Design (Wales) Ebbw Vale.

Chapter one

Pins and Needles

Peter Ivan Nicholas Smith is a very long name. It belonged to a small boy with curly red hair and lots of freckles.

One day some friends noticed that P from Peter, I from Ivan, N from Nicholas and S from Smith spelt a word...PINS. So they started to call him Pins, and after a while, so did everyone else.

"'Pins' suits you," said his dad, "because you are so sharp."

Pins felt his head, his toes, his ears, his nose... No part of his body felt *sharp*.

"Where?" he asked.

His dad laughed, "*Not* on the *outside*. You have a sharp mind – you're a 'thinking boy'. You ask a lot of questions."

As well as asking questions, Pins liked to paint and draw. Mostly, he painted and drew animals. He *wished* he could have a pet himself, but the flat where he lived had a very strict rule: NO PETS ALLOWED.

One evening Pins looked outside at a beautifully coloured sky and said, "*I* think God likes to paint pictures, too. It looks like he's painting one now, in the sky. Please can I go out and watch?"

"I'll come, too," said his dad.

They sat together on the garden seat, watching the sunset.

Dad said, "*I* think all the beautiful things God has put in the world are to help us remember he loves us."

"I *like* God," said Pins.

After a while, Pins's dad went inside to help Mum with the dishes.

"You can stay there till I call you, Pins," he said.

Pins started counting the colours in the sunset – red, orange, yellow...

Suddenly, a squeaky voice spoke from beneath the garden seat, "Hummph! I can't see why they call you *Pins*. There's not a prickle on you!"

"Who said that? Where are you?" gasped Pins.

"Me, and I'm down here," answered the squeaky voice. "Please be careful where you put those big bare feet. If you trod on me, it wouldn't be very nice for either of us."

Pins peered at the ground. Peering back up at him was a small, prickly hedgehog.

"I don't believe it! Hedgehogs can't talk!" Pins cried.

"Oh, *no*?" squealed the hedgehog, looking even pricklier, "Then how can you hear me?"

"I must be d-dreaming," stammered Pins.

"Perhaps you should prick yourself to find out if you're awake," said the hedgehog. "You haven't any prickles though, have you? I could do it for you, if you like."

"No, thanks!" answered Pins, moving back hurriedly.

"Why are you called Pins?" asked the hedgehog.

"It's made up from my real name," Pins explained. "Dad says it suits me because I'm sharp."

"Sharp?" squealed the hedgehog. "How can a small boy be *sharp*? Hedgehogs are sharp, because *we* have sharp prickles. Are you hiding your sharp prickles under your clothes?"

"Of course not," giggled Pins. "Dad says it means I'm a 'thinking boy'."

"Hmmm," said the hedgehog, "Well, think about *this*, 'thinking boy'. *My* name is Needles. Do you think because our names – Pins and Needles – are so alike, that *we* could be friends? Hmm?"

"*I* think I'd like that VERY MUCH," said Pins.

Chapter two

Rules and Rhymes

Pins was always asking his mum and dad questions. Now he was asking *all* about hedgehogs.

"What do hedgehogs EAT, Dad?"

"Snails and slugs, and beetles and bugs," answered his dad.

Pins didn't much like the thought of that.

"Hedgehogs like cat-food as well," said his mum.

That sounded a little better.

"Could we buy some, please?" asked Pins.

"Buy some *hedgehogs?*" grinned Dad.

"No – some *catfood*," giggled Pins.

"We don't mind you feeding a hedgehog, Pins, but remember it *mustn't* come into the flat," said Mum.

"I'll remember," promised Pins.

So Mum wrote 'cat-food' on her shopping list.

"Hedgehogs are good to have in the garden," said Dad. "They eat the bugs that eat our plants."

"It's a pity they don't *stay* in the garden, where they're safe," said Mum. "They wander on to the roads, and they don't know their road-safety rules."

"*I* can remember my road-safety rules," said Pins, proudly.

"Then you'd better teach the road-safety rules we've taught you, to the hedgehogs," joked Dad.

Pins thought... *I* could tell Needles about road-safety rules, and he could teach the other hedgehogs...

That evening, Pins rushed down to the garden seat.

Needles was already there.

"Needles," said Pins, "I have to tell you how to cross a road."

"*Anyone* can cross a *road*," sniffed Needles.

"But you need to know how to do it *safely*," said Pins. "You have to use your eyes, and ears."

"*I* use my *feet* when I cross a road," said Needles.

Pins giggled. "So do I, of course, but *first* I use my eyes and ears. Mum and Dad taught me this...

STOP before you cross a street
LOOK with your eyes
LISTEN with your ears, then
HURRY with your feet."

"I *like* that. It's very good," said Needles. "But you've left something out... Hedgehogs are better at smelling than seeing. How about this?

STOP before you cross a street
LOOK with your eyes
LISTEN with your ears
SNIFF with your snout
SHAKE your head about, then
HURRY with your feet."

Pins laughed. "Let's practise it together..."
So they did. Over and over. They even made up some actions!
"Will you remember it now?" asked Pins.
"I couldn't possibly forget it!" answered Needles.

"And, will you *do* it?" asked Pins.

"I'll do it," promised Needles.

"*And*, will you teach it to the other hedgehogs?" asked Pins.

"I will," said Needles.

Pins felt very happy to think he might have helped lots of hedgehogs to keep safe on the roads. He wondered if Noah had felt this way when he'd saved so many animals from the big flood, in his ark... *God* told Noah to look after those animals, Pins thought... I really, *really* like God...

Pins suddenly remembered the cat-food.

"Wait here, Needles," he said, and dashed inside.

Mum spooned some cat-food into a dish for Needles.

"Come straight inside after you've fed your hedgehog, Pins," she said.

Needles started gobbling straight away..

"Thanksh, Pinsh, thish ish *sho* yummy," he mumbled. "Won't you have shome yourshelf?"

Chapter three

Rain and Rainbows

"Mum, it's stopped raining!" called Pins. "Can I go out and play in the garden? *Please*."

Mum stared through the window at the sky.

"All right, Pins, but if the rain starts again, come straight inside."

"*Thanks*, Mum."

Pins wriggled into his jacket and boots. Then he picked up his school-bag.

He rushed splish-splash through the puddles and squish-squelch across the lawn, to the garden seat.

"If the feet in those boots belong to the boy I think they do, *what's kept you so long*?" squeaked a voice from beneath the seat.

"Mum made me stay inside," said Pins. "Didn't *your* mother make you stay somewhere dry till the rain had stopped?"

"I've lived on my own since I was six weeks old!" snorted Needles. "Nobody tells *me* when to come and go. We hedgehogs grow up *quickly*."

"Oh," said Pins. "I thought you might like to play a game, but it sounds like you're too grown-up."

"Being grown-up doesn't mean I can't have a bit of fun now and then," said Needles quickly. "What are we going to play ?"

"Sailing boats," said Pins. "We need the biggest puddle we can find."

"There's a big one under the apple tree," said Needles.

The puddle under the apple tree looked just right.

Pins opened up his school-bag.

"Nice bag," said Needles. "Is it new?"

"I haven't had it very long," answered Pins.

"What's inside it?" asked Needles curiously.

"Boats," answered Pins. "Mum showed me how to make them. I've made lots while it's been raining..."

Pins pulled the boats from his bag.

They were made from small boxes, and had paper sails which he'd painted all different colours.

"*Very* nice," squeaked Needles.

"I'll count them," said Pins. "I can count up to ten...One – two – three – four – five – six – *seven* boats! Now we'll put them in the water. The boat that floats for the longest time will be the winner."

Three boats fell over as soon as they went into the water.

Two boats drifted into each other, and sank.

There were only two boats still afloat.

"Let's call the big boat 'Noah's Ark'," said Pins. "That must have been the BIGGEST boat in the whole world. My mum and dad told me about it. God saved some of every sort of animal from a big flood, in Noah's Ark. Did you know there were two hedgehogs on that boat?"

"Really?" said Needles. "Er – who *is* God?"

"You haven't heard about God?" gasped Pins. "He's the one who made *everything*. He even made hedgehogs!"

"*Really?*" squeaked Needles. "Oh – look, Pins. The other boat is sinking. Noah's Ark has won!"

But Pins was busy looking at something else.

"Needles, LOOK AT THE SKY. See that rainbow? Dad says that God puts it there to tell us there won't ever be another big flood over all the earth. Look at all those different colours... *I'm* going to try and count them...

One – two – three – four – five – six – *seven*!"

Chapter four

Bikes and Bushes

"What shall we do tonight?" asked Needles.

"Dad mended my bike," said Pins, pointing. "See..."

"Yippee!" cheered Needles. "I've always wanted to ride one of those!"

Pins giggled. "I don't think your feet would reach the pedals. I've fixed this basket on to the handle-bars for you. It used to be on Mum's bike. It doesn't fit on mine very well, but I think it will do.."

"It will DO *very* nicely," squeaked Needles excitedly. "Help me in, please, Pins. If you wrap something round me, my prickles won't prick you."

Pins scooped Needles up in his jacket and bundled him into the basket.

"Stand-by for take-off!" he shouted, and pedalled down the wide concrete drive.

"Wheeee," squealed Needles. "This is FUN."

Pins turned around when they reached the gate, and rode back up the drive again.

Up and down they rode, going faster and faster.

After a while Needles called, "You *are* being careful, aren't you, Pins? It would be AWFUL to run someone over."

"There's nobody around!" yelled Pins.

"But Pins, some animals come out in the evenings, like *hedgehogs*," pointed out Needles.

At that very moment, a cat darted out from under a bush and ran *right in front of the bike.*

Pins grabbed his brakes, but the basket got in the way. The bike swerved. Needles flew into the air. The bike skidded to a wobbly stop.

"Needles! Are you all right?" called Pins, looking about for his hedgehog friend.

There was no answer.

Pins peered all around.

He couldn't see Needles *anywhere.*

"NEEDLES," he yelled. "Where *are* you?"

"On the moon, I think," answered a faraway voice.

Pins blinked. What did Needles mean? He couldn't possibly be on *the moon*!

Where WAS he?

"Tell me about the moon, Needles," Pins called, hoping this might lead him to the little hedgehog.

"It's evening here. It's rather cool," answered Needles. "I'm all alone, in the middle of something leafy.."

Something *leafy*? thought Pins, staring all

around... Then, suddenly, he worked it out...

"*Needles*," he yelled, "*you're on top of a bush.*"

"Am I?" squeaked Needles. "A *bush*? On *the moon*?"

"No," laughed Pins. "A bush in our garden! Look above you. There's the moon, just coming out now..."

"Oh," sighed Needles, very disappointed, "then I'm *not* the first hedgehog to land on the moon?"

"No, you're not," giggled Pins. "But you're probably the first hedgehog to land on that bush! Now, how am I going to get you down? You're too high up for me to reach you."

"No problem," said Needles. "I'll jump."

"It's too far!" gasped Pins.

"Not for a hedgehog," boasted Needles. "Not only do my prickles protect me from animals like cats and dogs and ferrets, they also help me to land safely when I jump or fall."

There was a soft thud, and a prickly ball landed at Pins's feet.

"See?" said Needles, unrolling and stretching. "Prickles are *useful*."

Pins was busy thinking again...

"*God* gave you your prickles, Needles," he said. "He made you that way, specially..

God thought of *everything*..."

Chapter five

Leaves and Leaving

Pins felt as gloomy as the grey autumn morning... Not even the sight of brightly-coloured autumn leaves could cheer him up. He shuffled his feet slowly through the fallen leaves that lay heaped on the ground... swish-swash, swish-swash, swish...

"Eeee!" squealed a voice from the middle of a pile of leaves, and Needles stumbled out, looking very sleepy and sounding *very* cross.

"So *you're* the one with the big clumsy feet!" he snorted. "You woke me up in the middle of a lovely dream, and look! LOOK what you've done *to my cosy nest* !"

"Was that pile of leaves your nest?" gasped Pins. "*Sorry*, Needles. I didn't know. I'll help you put it together again."

"Don't worry," mumbled Needles. "I'm too tired to wait around. I'm going away to another of my nests," and he started wandering off.

"Needles, stop! I have to tell you something! *I'm* going away, too," called Pins.

"That's good," grunted Needles. "I'll be able to sleep without worrying about *your feet.*"

Then he stopped, turned around, and squinted back at Pins.

"What do you mean, *going away*? You're not leaving *this place*, are you?"

Pins nodded. "We're all leaving. We're moving into a house – a proper house, with a really big garden. There's even a tree-swing... but, Needles, I *don't* want to leave YOU."

"I don't want you to leave me, either," said Needles. "Where is this house?"

"Not very far away. I won't have to change schools, so I'll still see my friends... except *you.*"

Needles yawned. "I won't be around for much longer myself, anyway, Pins. I'll be off *very* soon, to *hibernate.*"

Pins stared at him in surprise.

"To HIBERNATE? Where's *that*?"

"Perhaps you *should* change schools," squeaked Needles. "*Hibernate* isn't a *place*. It's a thing that hedgehogs do, when we go to sleep through the winter. Er – before an animal hibernates, it's good for him to eat a lot. The fat on his body helps to keep him warm. Um – I think, perhaps, I could be a little fatter... what do *you* think?"

"*I* think there might be some cat-food left in the fridge," said Pins.

"I was hoping you'd think that," yawned Needles happily. "Pleassse hurry Pinss... I'm soooo sssleepy."

Pins rushed inside. "Mum – please could I have some cat-food for my hedgehog? He's going to hibernate."

"*That's* a big word for you, Pins," said Dad in surprise.

Pins ran back to Needles with the catfood.

"Thank svery mush," mumbled the little hedgehog, slurping his meal in dreamy delight. But soon he was falling asleep in the dish.

"Walk with me to my nesht, Pinsh," he yawned, stumbling towards the hedge. "Is sunder here." Needles snuggled into a hollow beneath the hedge. Pins helped cover him with leaves.

"Bye, Needles," he called. But Needles was already fast asleep.

Pins felt sad. He hoped Needles would be all right. Then he remembered a Bible story his dad had read him, about how God watched over the sparrows...

"Dear God," he whispered, "I know you watch over the sparrows... please watch over Needles as well. Thank you. And, God, I really really like the way you made hedgehogs."

Chapter six

Many Happy Returns

Pins leaned his new skateboard against a tree. He wriggled on to the tree-swing and started gently swinging. It was a beautiful spring evening, and the garden of his new home was bright with flowers.

"There's only *one thing* missing," Pins sighed aloud.

"Would that be ME?" squeaked a voice from below the swing.

"NEEDLES!" cried Pins, tumbling off the swing so fast he nearly landed on top of the little hedgehog. "Is that *really you*? How did you *find* me?"

"I told you we hedgehogs are better at smelling than seeing," sniffed Needles. "I just followed my snout. You humans have a very strong scent. I could smell you from four streets away!"

Pins giggled. "I'm SO glad you found me, Needles. How are you?"

"How *am* I?" squeaked Needles. "I've been sleeping *all winter*. I'm *hungry...starving*...my legs are so weak they can hardly carry me...er, I don't suppose you could think of something to help, could you?"

"We didn't buy any more cat-food," said Pins. "I didn't know I'd be seeing you again...How about sausage? It's my birthday today, and we had a barbecue."

"Isn't a sausage one of those long fat meaty things humans eat, that looks a bit like a giant slug? I wouldn't mind trying one of those," answered Needles eagerly. "I wonder if it tastes like slug."

"I'll go and ask Mum if I can have one for you," said Pins, suddenly feeling as if he didn't like sausage very much. "You won't go near my new skateboard, will you?"

Pins dashed inside... "Mum, could I please have some sausage for my hedgehog?"

"I thought your hedgehog was hibernating, back at our old flat," said Mum.

"He was. But he's woken up. And he's here, and he's AWFULLY HUNGRY," said Pins.

"How would you know that? Have you been *talking* to him?" teased Dad.

"Anyone would be hungry after sleeping all winter," said Mum, slicing a cold sausage into pieces.

"Thanks, Mum." Pins hurried back along the path, watching the dish of sausages carefully.

Suddenly – *whizzzzzzPLOP!!!* he was lying flat on his back, with his new skateboard, wheels whirring, across his stomach, and slices of sausage scattered all over the lawn...

How had that skateboard got on the

path? And *where* was the little hedgehog whose legs had been too weak to carry him?

"*NEEDLES!*" yelled Pins. "*What* were you doing with my *skateboard*?"

"Oooooh," moaned Needles. "I feel so weak...so faint...ahhhhh..."

"All that sausage, all over the lawn," muttered Pins, picking a slice of sausage out of his hair.

"Did you say *sausage*?" squeaked Needles, bouncing back to life again. "Don't worry about the lawn, Pins. I'll clean it up. Um – Pins, what is it you humans say when you've done something wrong, to make it right?"

"We say we're sorry," answered Pins.

"Shorry about your shkateboard, Pinsh," mumbled Needles, busily munching. "Thanksh very mush for the shlug – I mean *shaushage* – and, MANY HAPPY RETURNSH!"

Chapter seven

Needles Speedles

Pins was putting knives and forks away in the drawer. He was in such a hurry, that he nearly put the forks in the space where the knives were meant to go.

"Please can I play outside on my new skateboard, now?" he asked.

"As long as you stay inside the gate," said Dad, smiling. "We're glad you're enjoying it so much."

Needles was already waiting under the tree-swing.

"Green grasshoppers!" he cheered. "You've remembered the skateboard. When can we start my driving lessons?"

Pins looked puzzled.

"But *I* thought, yesterday..."

"Oh, I wasn't *on* it, then – only pushing from behind – er, very weakly," stammered Needles.

Pins laughed behind his skateboard.

"Come on, then. The front drive is the best place to practise," he said, leading the way.

Pins set the skateboard down on the wide concrete drive.

"Climb aboard, Needles," he said. "I'll push you."

Needles scrambled on to the skateboard excitedly.

"Let's pretend," he said. "I'll be the racing-car driver, and you be the starter-man. Check the wheels, starter-man."

"One – two – three – four," counted Pins. "All there... ready to go."

"You're supposed to wave a flag," said Needles.

Pins pulled a clean handkerchief from his pocket.

"Ready, Needles Speedles?" he cried, waving the hanky above his head.

Down flashed the flag.

Pins grabbed the back of the skateboard and started pushing, slowly and carefully. Up and down the drive they went, while Needles practised how to balance and steer.

"I've learnt how to drive," said Needles, after a while. "Now I want to try by myself. Give me a huge push, Pins – then let go."

"I don't think you should do that," said Pins.

"*I* give the orders in this team, remember?" squeaked Needles. "*I'm* in the driver's seat. *You're* just the starter-man."

"All right, Needles Speedles," said Pins, "but I *did* warn you. Get ready for take-off!"

Pins grabbed the skateboard. He *PUSHED* with all his might – then let go.

"Oooooo... aaahhhh!" squealed Needles, as the skateboard rocketed forward. His clawed feet slid about, trying to get a grip on the smooth surface.

"Lean to the *other side*!" yelled Pins. "You're steering straight for the cherry tree!"

But Needles was too busy trying to stay on board to watch where he was going...

The skateboard zoomed off the drive, leapt across the lawn and crashed into the trunk of the flowering cherry tree. Needles flew up into the branches.

"Help, Pins! Get me out of here!" he squealed, as startled bees buzzed out from the blossoms. Dad's wheelbarrow was nearby. Quickly Pins wheeled it beneath the cherry tree. Then climbing in carefully, he reached up to where the little hedgehog was wedged between two branches, and gently wriggled him free.

"*Whew!*" gasped Needles, dropping safely on to the ground. "I could have got stung by a bee!"

"*I* could have got stung, too," pointed out Pins.

"You're *so brave*, Pins. You helped me out of trouble even after I didn't listen to you," said Needles.

"So I did," said Pins, thinking about it. "God does that – he helps people in trouble. Mum and Dad told me that... I really like God."

Chapter eight

Swinging and Singing

"Swing...ing, swing...ing,
Makes me feel like sing...ing,"

sang Pins, as he swung back and forth on
the swing that hung from a branch of the
big oak tree.

Needles watched from under the apple tree nearby.

"I wish *I* could do that," he sighed.

"Do what?" asked Pins. "Sing?"

"No..." snorted Needles. "*Anyone* can sing! I *WISH* I could SWING..."

Pins slowed down and slid off the swing.

"Here, Needles – have a turn. I'll help you up," he offered.

Needles squinted at the swing seat. It was made from a smooth, flat board.

"No thanks," he grunted. "I think I'd have the same problem I had on the skateboard – my feet wouldn't be able to hold on."

Pins sat back on the swing, and thought. He looked at Needles. He looked at the apple tree.

"Wait here, Needles," he said at last, and ran into the house.

After a while he returned. In one hand he was carrying a long silk scarf, that he'd found in Mum's drawer. In the other hand were some large safety-pins Mum usually stored with the bandages.

Needles watched curiously while Pins

looped the scarf over a low branch of the apple tree. Some curious bees buzzed out from the apple blossoms to watch, too, then flew off to find more flowers.

Pins carefully pinned the two loose ends of the scarf together with the large safety-pins.

"There!" he said, standing back and smiling. "A swing for a hedgehog. How do you like it?"

"*BRILLIANT*," cried Needles. "Can I try it?"

The scarf-swing hung so close to the ground Needles was able to scramble up into it with just a little help from Pins. With Needles's weight in the scarf, it drooped even lower.

"You wouldn't have far to go if you fell out of *there*," said Pins, giggling.

But there was no chance of Needles falling out – he fitted snugly into the looped scarf and his prickles clung to the soft material.

"Brilliant!" cried Needles again. "Could you push my swing, please Pins, to start me swinging?"

Pins grabbed the sides of the scarf and set it swinging.

"*Higher! Faster!*" called Needles.

"That's high and fast enough," said Pins.

He ran to the oak tree and climbed on his own swing.

Pins and Needles swung and sang together, each from his own swing in his own tree...

> "Swing...ing, swing...ing,
> Makes me feel like sing...ing..."

Then Needles made up this verse...

> "Swing...swing, swing...swing,
> Thank you for my swing-thing.."

And Pins made up *this one*...

"Tree...dles, Spee...dles
Thank you, God, for *Needles*.."

How Pins draws hedgehogs.

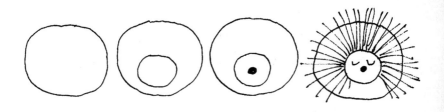

How Pins made Needles's swing.

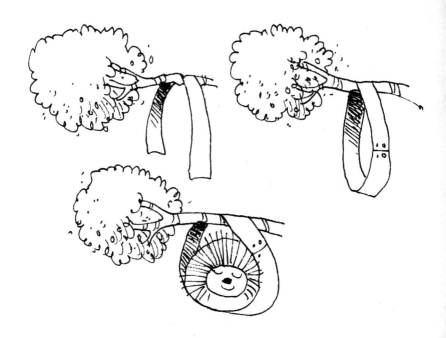

Chapter nine

Sour Fruit

Pins climbed out of bed and pulled Mum's scarf from his school-bag. It looked even worse than it had the night before. Pins felt really worried... What was Mum going to say when she saw all the holes made by Needles's prickles?

All day long Pins felt *bad*. He didn't want to even look at his parents. At mealtimes, it was hard work making words come out, and food go down.

Evening came at last. Pins rushed out to share his problem with his hedgehog friend.

"What's wrong? You've got a face like a sour apple," squeaked Needles.

"Mum's *scarf*," groaned Pins, reaching inside his jacket and pulling out the torn scarf.

"Uh-oh," gulped Needles, staring. "That's not just a lacey pattern, is it?"

"More like a *prickle* pattern," moaned Pins.

"Oops," said Needles. "What did your mum say?"

"She doesn't know I borrowed it," answered Pins miserably. "I took it without asking."

"Uh-oh," muttered Needles again.

"What can I DO?" wailed Pins.

"Why don't you do what you told me humans usually do, to make things right when they've done something wrong?" said Needles. "Tell her you're sorry – then you can be friends again."

Pins thought for a long time.

"That's what I need to do," he said at last. "That's what God would want me to do, too – to tell the truth, and say I'm sorry..."

"It could change everything – even the look on your face!" said Needles.

"I'll do it!" said Pins bravely.

He marched up the path to the house...one-two, one-two...up the steps...one-two, one-two...in through the door...one-two, one-

"Whatever's the matter, Pins?" asked Mum.. "You look like you've eaten a lemon!"

Pins gulped. He held out the torn scarf.

"I'm s-sorry," he stammered. "I t-took it without asking, and it got t-torn."

Mum stared. "It certainly did! It looks like it's been tangled-up in a rose bush! Come here, Pins. I can see you're really sorry ... so let's put that old rag in the rubbish, eh? There. It's gone. Now, let's forget about it."

Pins and Mum gave each other a big hug. Then Pins dashed back outside to tell Needles the good news. But his smiling face told Needles first.

"That's a *much* better face!" squeaked Needles. "I can see saying 'sorry' *really works*."

PINS'S DRAWINGS

Pins drew something. "Guess what *this* is.." he said.

"A cloud?" said Mum.
"Hills?" said Dad.
Pins drew some more.
"Guess what it is now.."

"A car with four flat tyres?" said Dad.
"I've no idea," said Mum.
Pins quickly added something else.

"It's A HEDGEHOG!" shouted Mum and Dad together. "That's *very clever*, Pins."

Chapter ten

Ups and Downs

The trampoline arrived in a van. It had once belonged to Pins's cousins, but they had outgrown it. Pins watched excitedly as Dad and Mum and the van-driver set it down near his 'swing-tree'.

Dad thanked and paid the van-driver, and he left.

"Well, Pins, aren't you going to slip your shoes off and try the trampoline?" smiled Dad.

Pins climbed up.

"There's a trampoline at my school," he said. "I've learned how to do 'knees' and 'bottoms'. Watch!"

"Whew!" whistled Dad. "Great stuff, Pins. Do you think *I* could learn how to do that?"

Dad had a try.

Then Mum had a turn.

"Remember, Pins, when your friends come to play, you must all take turns," said Mum.

"I'll remember," said Pins. He could hardly wait for one *special* friend to try his trampoline.

Evening arrived at last, and so did Needles.

"What's this table for?" Needles squeaked excitedly, staring up at the trampoline. "Are we having a *party*?"

"It's a *trampoline*," laughed Pins. "It's for jumping on – not for *eating off*... watch!" Needles watched.

"*My turn! My turn!*" he squealed excitedly.

"I've been thinking about how you could climb up there..." said Pins. "If I leaned a tree-branch against the trampoline, do you think you could climb up that?"

"No problem," answered Needles.

Pins glanced around the garden. Dad had been trimming the trees – there *should* be a branch the right length *somewhere*...

While Pins was looking for a branch, Needles made a quick trip to the vegetable garden.

"There's a whole family of slugs under this cabbage!" he called. "Shall I bring you one?"

"*NO THANKS!*" shouted Pins. "Hurry up, Needles. I've found you a branch!"

Needles waddled back looking plump and pleased.

"Try climbing up this," said Pins. "I'll hold it steady."

Needles clambered up the branch to the trampoline, puffing and panting.

"You shouldn't have filled up your tummy," giggled Pins. "Then you wouldn't have had so much to carry..."

"It may have been hard work for me to get up, but I'm better than you are at getting down!" sniffed Needles.

"How about moving to the middle of the trampoline, and trying some 'ups' *and* 'downs'?" said Pins.

Needles scampered to the middle of the trampoline, and jumped.

"It's *not working*," he wailed. "I'm not bouncing up *high*. Can you make me bounce high, Pins? *Please.*"

Pins slipped his shoes off and climbed up. "Watch where you put your feet!" warned Needles.

"Don't worry – I *will*," said Pins, beginning

to bounce gently.

"*Wheeee!*" cried Needles.

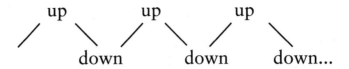

Bigger bounces, Pins. *Bigger! BIGGER!*
Wheeee...*I'm FLYING...*

up ⌣ up ⌣ up ⌣ up ⌣ up ⌣ up
  down   down hicc hicc hicc

ooooooooo... st- st- st- *stop-p-p.*"

Pins stopped.
"I don't feel very w-well," moaned
Needles. "M-maybe hedgehogs weren't
meant to fly."
"*Especially* one with a full tummy!" Pins
giggled. "God made you into a hedgehog,
not *a bird* – and I like you *just the way he
made you.*"
"Really?" squeaked Needles happily. "I
kind of like the way he made you, too!"

Chapter eleven

Ins and Outs

One morning at breakfast Mum announced, "I've had enough. That hedgehog will *have* to go."

Pins dropped his spoon with a clatter.

Mum yawned. "It's been keeping me awake, rustling about outside the house at night."

"A hedgehog's good to have if it stays in the garden," said Dad. "I've noticed there are fewer slugs and snails eating our vegetables."

"*This* hedgehog *doesn't* stay in the garden," yawned Mum. "I'll give it two more nights, then I think we should look for a dog or cat. Pins has wanted a pet for a long time."

Pins gulped. If a cat or dog moved in, Needles would *certainly* move out.

"Somebody had better warn that

hedgehog," Dad joked.

Somebody did! That evening Pins *r-a-c-e-d* outside.

"Needles!" he cried. "*Why* have you been snooping *around the house at night*?"

Needles sniffed. "Why have *you* been keeping *secrets* from me? *I* saw the animal you're hiding in the house through the window. It was crouching in a corner, making noises and changing colours *really fast*. But it couldn't fool *me*!"

Pins blinked. Then he laughed.

"Needles, that's *our television*. It isn't an animal! It isn't *alive*."

"It was alive last night," said Needles. "Didn't you feed it?"

"I'll *show* you the TV," said Pins. "I'll smuggle you inside somehow, if you *promise* to s*tay away* afterwards. If you don't, Mum's going to get a cat or dog to *keep you away*!"

"Aaahhh!" squealed Needles. "I'll be good. I promise."

Pins ran back inside and grabbed his school-bag. He glanced out of the window, and saw that his parents were out at the front gate, chatting to a friend. He zoomed back to Needles. "Quick, Needles! Mum and Dad are both outside.

Climb into my bag!"

Needles scrambled into the school-bag. Pins rushed down the hall to the sitting-room.

He put the bag down in front of the television. Needles clambered out.

"See, Needles? It *isn't* an animal. It works by *electricity*. Watch. I'm switching it on."

VOOM!!! The television sprang to life. A wild-life programme was showing. A large lion stared out at them – then, it opened its huge mouth and – *ROARED*.

"*AAAAHHHH!*" shrieked Needles, burrowing into the school-bag. "*CHASE IT AWAY!*"

Pins switched off the TV. "It's gone, Needles. It was only a picture!"

"Are you *SURE* it's gone?" shivered Needles. "Let's get out of here, *please*."

Pins suddenly heard his parents coming back in through the front door.

He snatched up his school-bag, and sped down the hall to the back door.

Just as they got there, Dad *sneezed* – *LOUDLY* – '*AH-AH-AH – CHOOOOO!!!*'

"Eeeeeee!" squealed Needles. "It's

AFTER US. Run, Pins, RUN!"

Pins ran out the door and down the path to the oak tree. Then he burst out laughing. "N-Needles... ha-ha-ha... *that* was just Dad... *SN-SNEEZING* ... ha-ha.."

"It *isn't* funny," sniffed Needles. "I'm *never* going near your house again!"

"Good," smiled Pins. "I'd *much rather* have *you* for a friend than a cat or dog!"

"Me, too," agreed Needles. "And, Pins, I'm glad God made us different. It's fun having a friend who's different."

"It sure is!" chuckled Pins. "God made everything *SO* well. I *REALLY* like God."

Chapter twelve

Thoughts and Fun

"Uh-oh... what's the matter *this* time?" asked Needles, as Pins dawdled down the path to the oak tree. "You look as lively as a snail with a prickle in its foot."

"I have to tell you some news I don't think you're going to like," answered Pins.

"Well, then? What is it?" squeaked Needles.

Pins told him. "We're going away, on holiday..."

"Squirmy worms!" cried Needles. "Are we *really*? Where are we going? When do we leave?" He glanced toward the vegetable garden. "Should I pack us a special picnic lunch?"

"No, Needles. *I'm* going, with Mum and Dad. *YOU'RE* not coming..."

"*Hmmph*!" sniffed Needles. "Well, off you go and enjoy yourself, then. No need to worry about *me*. I'll just stay here, in the same old place, doing all the same old things... "

"You don't *have* to do all the '*same old things*'," said Pins. "I've been thinking about that... The place where we're going has a *brilliant* playground – I thought I could make *you* a playground, too, right here, in our garden..."

"Could you *really*?" squeaked Needles. "A *playground*? I could be playing in *my* playground while you're playing in yours! It would be like a 'holiday at home'. Um – what sort of things will there be, to play on?"

"Well...," said Pins. "I'll leave the tree-branch against the trampoline so you can climb up and use that... and I asked Mum if I could have an old towel she was throwing away – I thought I could make you a new swing with that... "

"Great!" cried Needles. "What else? What else?"

"Dad's got three old boards he said I could use," answered Pins. "I'm going to make a slide with one, by leaning it against the trampoline, and I'm going to lay one across a brick to make a see-saw."

"What about the other one?" asked Needles excitedly.

"I'm hoping that will reach between the trampoline and the apple tree," said Pins, "to make a bridge for you to walk along. And the last thing is a piece of broken drain-pipe – that will be a tunnel for you to crawl through.."

"Such a lot of things!" squeaked Needles happily. "How many things, Pins? Can you count them?"

Pins counted.. "Trampoline...swing... slide... see-saw... bridge... tunnel – *six*!"

"When can you start making it?" asked Needles eagerly.

"Right now," said Pins. "I'll go and get the boards from Dad's shed, first. The bricks and broken drain-pipe are behind the shed."

Lastly, Pins ran inside for the old towel and some safety-pins. Then he started to put everything in place.

Needles watched excitedly.

"Have you nearly finished? Can I play in it now?" he kept asking.

Finally Pins answered, "It's all finished, Needles. You can play in your playground, now!"

"Wheeeee!" squealed Needles, scampering excitedly from one play-thing to another, then running back for a second turn at everything. "*Thanks ever so much*, Pins. This is such fun."

"*I* had fun, thinking it out and making it for you, too, Needles," said Pins.

Then, watching Needles enjoying his playground, Pins thought to himself...

I wonder if God had fun, thinking out and making the world for us?